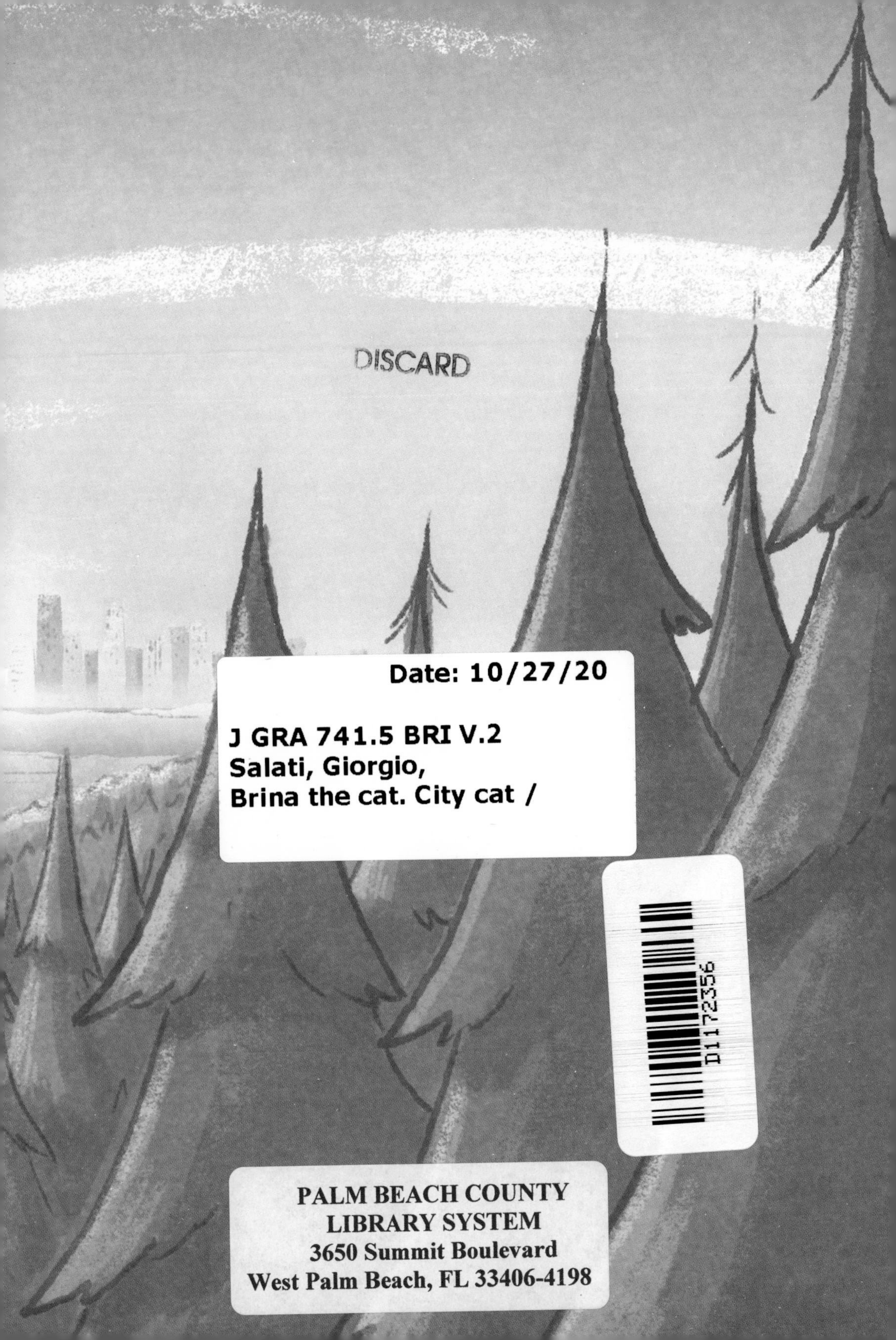

GIORGIO SALATI

CHRISTIAN CORNIA

BRINA the CAT

PAPERCUTZ

MORE GREAT GRAPHIC NOVEL SERIES AVAILABLE FROM PAPERCUT

THE SMURFS

THE ONLY LIVING GIRL

THE ONLY LIVING BOY

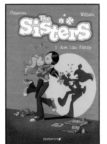

THE SISTERS

CAT & CAT

GERONIMO STILTON

THEA STILTON

GERONIMO STILTON REPORTER

DINOSAUR EXPLORERS

GEEKY FAB 5

FUZZY BASEBALL

THE MYTHICS

THE RED SHOES

THE LITTLE MERMAID

BLUEBEARD

GILLBERT

THE LOUD HOUSE

MELOWY

ATTACK OF THE STUFF

GUMBY

papercutz.com

All available where ebooks are sold.

GIORGIO
SALATI

CHRISTIAN
CORNIA

BRINA the CAT

#2 CITY CAT

PAPERCUT Z

New York

To the girls and boys of all ages who have become
attached to Brina.
This book is for you.

–Giorgio and Christian

#2 "City Cat"
©2020 TUNUÉ (Tunué s.r.l) - Giorgio Salati and Christian Cornia
Originally published in Italy as *Brina 2. Ogni amico è un'avventura*
by TUNUÉ (Tunué s.r.l.) in 2020. All rights reserved. www.tunue.com
English translation and all other editorial material ©2020 by Papercutz.
www.papercutz.com

GIORGIO SALATI — Script
CHRISTIAN CORNIA — Art, Color, and Cover
MASSIMILIANO CLEMENTE — Original Editor
ALESSANDRO AURELI — Original Lettering and Layout

Special thanks to CECILIA RANERI

NANETTE McGUINNESS — Translation
JEFF WHITMAN —Editor, Lettering, Production
JIM SALICRUP
Editor-in-Chief

Papercutz books may be purchased for business or promotional use.
For information on bulk purchases please contact
Macmillan Corporate and Premium Sales Department at
(800) 221-795 x5442.

Hardcover ISBN: 978-1-5458-0496-4
Paperback ISBN: 978-1-5458-0497-1

Printed in India
June 2020

Distributed by Macmillan
First Papercutz Printing

Chapter 1 : Homeward Bound

Vacation is over and now it's time for Brina, Margret, and Sam to head back to their own apartment in the city...

HOW ABOUT WE MAKE A PIT STOP?

SURE!

WHENEVER WE TAKE HER OUTSIDE, THE TRAFFIC SCARES HER.

WE'LL JUST BE A FEW MINUTES, BRINA...

SHALL WE LET THE CAT STRETCH HER LEGS?

YES, BUT INSIDE THE CAR.

AND DON'T YOU EVEN THINK ABOUT DRIVING OFF WITH THE CAR! HA! HA!

Brina is content just exploring inside...

TRAVELING IS SO BORING! I CAN'T WAIT TO GET HOME.

... But then, an uninvited guest breaks in...

?

... and our feline heroine is forced into hiding...

HA! UNLOCKING A CAR'S NEVER BEEN EASIER.

I WONDER HOW MUCH I CAN GET FOR THIS JUNKHEAP?

If Brina doesn't do something, she'll soon be separated from Sam and Margret.

MEOWRRR!

WHAT THE--?!

HISSSSSS!

HELP!

SINCE WHEN DID CARS START HAVING GUARD CATS IN THEM?

Brina's misadventure is just beginning, as the robber neglected to properly put the car in park...

... and the car starts rolling downhill.

HOW DOES THIS THINGIE STOP?

HOW LONG UNTIL WE TURN?

OH, I DON'T KNOW, VINCENT. I CAN'T READ ANYTHING ON THIS DARN MAP?

?

D-DEAR, DID YOU SEE THAT?

A CAT WAS JUST DRIVING THAT CAR THERE!

AT LEAST IT WASN'T ANOTHER JACKASS.

HOW MANY TIMES HAVE I TOLD YOU, VINCENT? YOU MUST BE WELL RESTED BEFORE GETTING BEHIND THE WHEEL!

OH, NO!

The situation gets worse and worse. Brina and the car head towards a cliff at full speed.

MEOOW!

KAKLANG

WHAT WAS THAT RACKET?

MAYBE I SHOULD STOP AND CHECK IT OUT.

Luckily, the car carrier trailer brings Brina right back to where this adventure began.

LET'S LOOK AROUND A BIT.

THE TIRES SEEM GOOD AND FULL.

Brina has to get out of there, but attracting attention is no easy task.

MEOOOW!

MEOOOW!

EVERYTHING'S OKAY HERE TOO...

CAN'T BELIEVE I IMAGINED THE WHOLE DARN THING. THAT'S IT! I NEED TO RETIRE SOON...

PLEASE DON'T LEAVE! I WANT TO GET BACK TO MY FAMILY!

OOPS!

BEEEP

SOMEONE UP THERE HONKED!

I DON'T KNOW WHAT THIS NOISE IS, BUT IT'S MY ONLY HOPE!

BEEEP BEEEP BEEEP

BEEEP

BEEEP

WHERE'D THAT CAR COME FROM?

AND MORE IMPORTANTLY, WHO HONKED THAT HORN?

THAT'S THE FIRST TIME I'VE SEEN A GHOST CAR.

WILL YOU LOOK AT THAT? IT WAS A CAT!

I'LL CHECK THE LOG. I DON'T THINK I HAD THIS CAR ON BOARD, MUCH LESS THAT CAT.

Sam and Marge will never know what Brina went through.

DOES IT SEEM LIKE THE CAR'S MOVED TO YOU?

DID YOU SET THE PARKING BREAK?

I'M SURE I DID...

YOU COULDN'T HAVE MOVED IT, BRINA, RIGHT?

IF YOU WANT TO DRIVE, AT LEAST WAIT UNTIL YOU HAVE A LICENSE!

Once again, Brina the cat braved dangers to stay with her family.
And now, the journey can begin again...

JUST AS I THOUGHT: ACCORDING TO THE LOG, THAT CAR ISN'T THERE.

ACTUALLY... IT ISN'T HERE!

SO THEN... WAS IT REALLY A GHOST CAR? ...AND A GHOST CAT?

And so, we leave the truck driver with her doubts...

... and Brina with a new realization.

WELL... I CAN'T DRIVE, BUT NOW I'M A PRO AT MAKING NOISE TO GET SOMEONE'S ATTENTION!

With their mountain adventures over, it's time for Brina, Margret, and Sam to return to the city.

WE'RE HOME.

I ALREADY MISS THE FRESH MOUNTAIN AIR.

WE'LL GO BACK SOON, YOU'LL SEE...

I'LL GO PARK THE CAR.

OKAY.

I'LL BE RIGHT THERE, BRINA... I'M GOING TO GO CHECK THE MAIL.

Returning to city life isn't very adventurous for Brina.

≥YAWN.≤

... but if it's adventure the feline's looking for, she'll soon get her wish.

WELL, LOOKY HERE.

WHAT'S THAT? A CAT IN A CAGE?

?

AND LOTSA BAGS!

MAYBE WE'LL FIND SOME FOOD.

WHAT'RE YOU DOING? DON'T TOUCH THAT!

WHO CARES? SHE'S IN NO POSITION TO MAKE DEMANDS.

WHAT DOES THAT CAT WANT?

There aren't many rules Brina claims to respect...

But one she does is: Brina's the only animal allowed to touch Sam and Margret's things.

HEY!

HA! HA!

OW!

14

WE'LL BE BACK, YOU NASTY CAT...

AND WE'LL GET REVENGE!

WHENEVER YOU WANT, I'LL BE HERE.

A special spectator had witnessed Brina's little victory over the rats: Falstaff, the local stray.

NICE MOVE, BRINA... BUT IT CAN BE DANGEROUS GETTING THE RATS MAD.

HI, FALSTAFF.

I'M NOT AFRAID OF THOSE RATS... I'VE FACED MUCH BIGGER DANGERS IN MY TIME IN THE WOODS.*

THE MAIL HASN'T COME YET THIS MORNING.

I SEE YOU'RE CATCHING UP WITH FALSTAFF.

IN THAT CASE, I'LL LEAVE YOU OUT HERE ANOTHER MINUTE WHILE I BRING UP THE LUGGAGE.

WELL... I'M OFF TO LOOK FOR FOOD. GOOD LUCK.

YOU TOO.

* SEE BRINA THE CAT #1 "THE GANG OF THE FELINE SUN"

If Falstaff had lingered just a few seconds longer, he would have seen an extraordinary scene...

UH-OH.

TAM TARATATAM TAM TAAAM!

... an imperial march sung by an army of rats in military gear.

MAKE WAY FOR HUFF, KING OF THE RATS!

SO, FELINE... I HEAR YOU DISRESPECTED MY BOYS.

YOUR "BOYS" DISRESPECTED THEMSELVES ON THEIR OWN.

BUT I DO APPRECIATE THE FUNNY STUNT THEY PULLED TO WELCOME ME BACK TO THE CITY.

IS THAT A JOKE? IS SHE KIDDING?

I THINK SO, BOSS.

ALRIGHT... GRAB THE CAT!

HEY!

LET'S SEE IF YOU'RE STILL LAUGHING SOON.

PUT ME DOWN!

16

MIGHT I ASK WHERE YOU'RE TAKING ME?

OBVIOUSLY TO OUR SECRET HIDEOU-- OW!

STUPID RAT! YOU'RE NOT SUPPOSED TO MENTION THAT. IT'S A SECRET.

YOU'RE STUPID! IF WE'RE TAKING HER THERE, HOW SECRET IS IT?

CUT IT OUT, YOU TWO!

YOUR FOLLOWERS DON'T SEEM VERY BRIGHT... THEN AGAIN, THEY'RE FOLLOWING YOU.

YOU KEEP QUIET TOO.

I'M GOING TO MAKE YOU STOP WANTING TO BE SUCH A SMART MOUTH.

HERE'S WHERE YOUR FATE WILL BE DETERMINED.

HALT!

WAIT HERE.

BUT BOSS... SHE'S HEAVY!

?

?

OKAY, YOU CAN COME UP!

WELCOME TO MY KINGDOM, CAT. HAVE A LOOK AROUND, IT'S THE LAST THING THAT YOU'RE GOING TO SEE.

WOW... THE BOSS GOT ALL DRESSED UP!

THINK THE BOSS WANTS TO IMPRESS THE CAT?

CUT IT OUT, CHEESE BREATH!

LET'S SEE, WHAT CAN I DO WITH YOU?

DEMAND A RANSOM FROM YOUR OWNER? TURN YOU INTO A THROW RUG?

I WOULDN'T TRUST YOUR FRIEND. HE LOOKS LIKE A TRAITOR.

HUH? YOU TALKING TO ME?

NO! SHE WAS TALKING TO ME!

SO, I'M THE TRAITOR?

AH, SO YOU ADMIT IT?

STOP THAT! I CAN'T EVEN THINK!

SO... COULD I ASK FOR THR RANSOM PAID IN CEREAL?

I REALLY COULD USE A NEW OLD SHOE TOO.

TELL US, WHO'S THE TRAITOR?

AH, IF YOU DIDN'T KNOW... SOMEONE'S LEAKED EVERYTHING!

EVERY-THING?

I KNEW I SMELLED A RAT!

Luckily for Brina, the rats squabble...

MAYBE IT'S YOU!

WHOEVER SAYS THAT KNOWS THEY'RE THE SPY!

... and don't watch her...

...then the cat spots a messenger passing by right below her.

A little push...

⸗HMF!⸗

19

... and he unknowingly gives her a lift!

STUPID RATS! SHE ESCAPED!

BUT, BOSS, HOW COULD WE KNOW THE CAT COULD FLY?

MAYBE IT WAS THE CAGE THAT FLEW?

Meanwhile, Margret and Sam are worried once again...

BUT HOW...? WASN'T SHE WITH YOU?

WHAT HAPPENED TO BRINA?

DELIVERY!

WHAT? YOU'VE GOT OUR CAT ON YOUR LUGGAGE RACK!

?

HOW'S THAT POSSIBILE?

WE DON'T KNOW...

... WE'RE JUST HAPPY THAT SHE'S BACK. WE DON'T EVER WANT TO LOSE HER AGAIN.

MEOW.

And that's how Brina discovered that nothing, not even a cage, could keep her from her family...

Returning from vacation was full of adventure, but Brina, Margret, and Sam are at last ready to cross their threshold...

FINALLY, THAT'S THE LAST BAG...

EVERY TIME WE GO ON VACATION, IT FEELS LIKE WE'VE MOVED!

THE IMPORTANT THING IS NOT TO FORGET BRINA!

OH, GOOD MORNING, MRS. TORVALDI.

HUH?

I SAID, "GOOD MORNING!"

AH... GOOD EVENING THEN!

AND HOW'S SWEET COLETTE DOING?

OH, YOU'RE LEAVING? OFF SKIING?

HUH? NO... SUMMER'S JUST ENDED. THERE'S NO SNOW...

PLEASE, GO AHEAD. WE WON'T ALL FIT IN THE ELEVATOR.

THANKS! ENJOY BOWLING!

POOR MRS. TORVALDI. SHE'S AT THAT AGE WHERE SHES' NOT ALWAYS THINKING CLEARLY...

YOU DON'T SAY...

I CAN'T WAIT TO OPEN UP THAT JAR OF ORGANIC HONEY FROM THE MOUNTAINS I'VE GOT IN MY SUITCASE.

WE'RE FINALLY HERE AT OUR FLOOR.

HEY!

WHAT'S GOING ON?

A PIGEON!

HOW'D IT GET IN OUR BUILDING?

AH!

BRINA! LEAVE HIM ALONE!

The uninvited bird flies up another floor, not knowing he's about to double his trouble... and other's too!

WOOF!

WOOF! WOOF!

COLETTE! MY WORD!

COLEEEEETTE!

THAT SOUNDS LIKE MRS. TORVALDI...

STOP... STOP IT, COLETTE!

THERE SHE IS... BEHIND THE PIGEON!

How can you tell the true nature of a cat? By their quick reflexes?

The elderly woman is headed for disaster and no one is quick enough to help her...

... except for a feline with a kind soul.

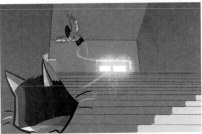

BRINA... SAVED MRS. TORVALDI!

ARE YOU OKAY, MA'AM?

I'M OKAY... BUT WHO ARE YOU? WHERE AM I?

HERE'S YOUR DOOR, MA'AM.

THANKS, VIRGIL.

UHM... MY NAME'S SAM.

NO, GABRIEL, I WON'T GIVE YOU A DIME.

COME, COLETTE, NO TALKING TO STRANGERS.

MERCY! I'M BEGGING YOU!

HAH! YOU'RE TRAPPED!

WHERE'D BRINA WIND UP?

I THINK SHE'S UP IN THE ATTIC.

I'VE GOT AN IDEA HOW TO GET HER TO COME BACK DOWN.

MY NAME'S PETER... IF YOU SPARE MY LIFE, I'LL FOREVER BE IN YOUR DEBT!

UHM...

BRINA? COME EAT!

I'VE GOT YOUR FAVORITE KIBBLE!

OKAY... WELL, GET ON OUT OF HERE. YOU'VE ALREADY MADE ENOUGH OF A MESS.

I DON'T KNOW HOW!

I GOT IN THROUGH A SLIT IN THE ROOF... BUT I CAN'T FIND IT AGAIN.

OKAY, LET'S LOOK FOR IT.

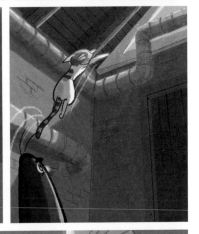

HERE IT IS!

THANK YOU! THANK YOU!

I'M FREEEE!

HERE'S OUR HEROINE!

YOU KNOW YOU WERE VERY BRAVE, RIGHT?

THE ELDERLY WOMAN UPSTAIRS COULD HAVE REALLY GOTTEN HURT AND YOU SAVED HER WITH THE SUITCASE.

THE CLOTHES SOFTENED THE BLOW AND... **OH, NO!**

MY... MY...

MY JAR OF HONEY!

Brina and Sam both learned something from this series of events...

... sometimes you must make sacrifices in order to help someone in trouble!

Chapter 4: The Hidden Terrace

A peaceful morning of doing nothing is what a house cat wants the most...

... except for a cat with an insatiable spirit for adventure.

MEOOOW!

WHAT'S GOING ON? IS BRINA HURT?

NO... SHE WANTS TO GO OUT.

OKAY... AFTER ALL, YOU CAN'T DO ANYTHING MORE THAN ROAM AROUND THE STAIRWELL.

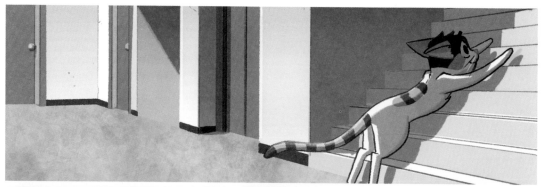

I WONDER IF I CAN FIND THAT HOLE IN THE ROOF AGAIN.

THERE IT IS!

And that's how, through a narrow opening, Brina found a part of the building she's never explored before.

The terrace!

The most exotic of terraces, inhabited by...

... parrots with gaudy colors in pairs...

...and one single, solitary gray parrot, looking quite sad and downtrodden.

HEY! HEY, FRIEND OUT THERE!

WHO? ME?

HELP ME GET OUT OF HERE! PLEASE? PLEASEPLEASE!

REALLY... I DON'T KNOW IF--

LOOK AT ME! MY FEATHERS ARE MOLTING BECAUSE I'M LOCKED UP ALL ALONE!

ACTUALLY, YOU DON'T LOOK ALL THAT... HEALTHY.

ALL THE OTHER PARROTS ARE PAIRED UP... MAYBE IF I GOT OUT OF HERE I COULD FIND A LIFE PARTNER FOR MYSELF.

SO FAR, MY ONLY COMPANY HAS BEEN SOMEONE'S TV FROM THE PENTHOUSE APARTMENT... BY NOW, I'VE LEARNED COMMON HUMAN EXPRESSIONS.

LISTEN TO THIS:

USE MOXI-BRITE AND YOUR TEETH WILL BE SUPER BRIGHT, ALRIGHT!

I THINK IT MUST BE A VERY IMPORTANT EXPRESSION, I HEAR IT ALL THE TIME.

YOU'RE FUNNY!

OKAY... I'LL HELP YOU GET OUT OF THERE.

=GNNN=...

THERE YOU GO.

I'M FREE!

THANK YOU, MY SAVIOR... NAME'S OLIVER.

I'M BRINA.

I'LL NEVER FORGET YOU, BRINA!

BUT... WHAT ARE YOU DOING?

'MORNING, BEAUTIFUL!

LEAVE ME ALONE!

BEG YOUR PARDON, I MISTOOK YOU FOR A LADY PARROT!

AHH!

AAHH!

OUCH...

NOW WHAT'S GOING ON?

I DIDN'T FREE THAT PARROT JUST TO HAVE HIM ROUGHED UP BY RATS!

HEY, PETER! REMEMBER HOW YOU OWE ME A FAVOR?

YES, UNFORTUNATELY... WHAT DO I HAVE TO DO?

The task Brina gives the poor pigeon isn't an easy one...

YOU'RE TOO HEAVY!

SAVE YOUR BREATH FOR FLYING...

... OR AT LEAST FALLING SLOWLY!

NONONONONO!

MEOW!

⇾PHEW⇽...
BY A TAIL
FEATHER!

I'M GOING
TO...

... FALL!

OUCH!

Y-YOU SAVED ME...
TWICE, BRINA! NO ONE'S
EVER DONE THIS MUCH FOR
ME BEFORE.

WELL... I COULDN'T
JUST STAND BY AND WATCH
THE RATS MANGLE A POOR,
DEFENSELESS ANIMAL!

#@$£%!

I THINK IT MAY BE BETTER
FOR ME TO RETURN TO MY
AVIARY FOR NOW.

YOU'RE LUCKY
YOU CAN FLY...
HOW WILL I GET
BACK HOME?

But strange
as it sounds, a
parrot and a
cat...

... can come up with
good ideas together...

SOMETIMES
WHEN HUMANS
WANT TO GO TO THEIR
KENNELS, THEY PRESS
THEIR PAWS ON THAT
THING THERE...

YES?

YOUR DREAM'S
COME TRUE,
THERE'S NOW A
SPLENDID MARKET
NEAR YOU!

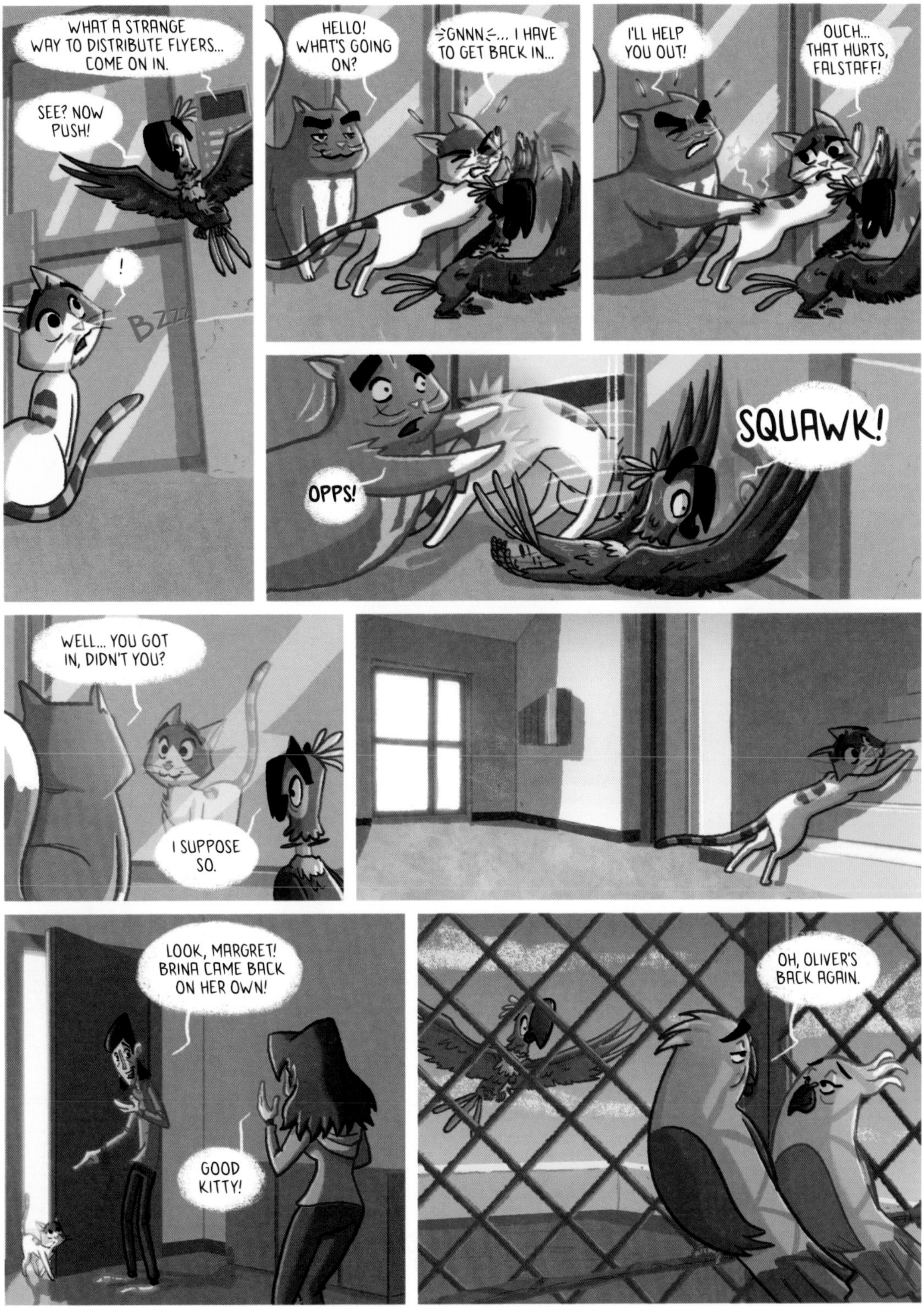
WHAT A STRANGE WAY TO DISTRIBUTE FLYERS... COME ON IN.
SEE? NOW PUSH!
!
BZZZ
HELLO! WHAT'S GOING ON?
GNNN... I HAVE TO GET BACK IN...
I'LL HELP YOU OUT!
OUCH... THAT HURTS, FALSTAFF!
OPPS!
SQUAWK!
WELL... YOU GOT IN, DIDN'T YOU?
I SUPPOSE SO.
LOOK, MARGRET! BRINA CAME BACK ON HER OWN!
GOOD KITTY!
OH, OLIVER'S BACK AGAIN.

YOUR ESCAPE IN SEARCH OF LOVE OVER ALREADY?

HA! HA!

WISE GUYS.

IN FACT, I EVEN MADE FRIENDS WITH OTHER SPECIES.

ANYWAYS, I'M SURE I'LL FIND MY SOULMATE SOONER OR LATER.

It's been a few hours since the mishap with the gray bird, and dusk has now fallen over the homes in the city...

"ENJOY TAMARIND'S SPECIAL BLEND...

?

"... AND MAKE YOURSELF A TASTY NEW FRIEND!"

IS THE TV ON, GIRL?

IT'S OFF... BUT I COULD HAVE SWORN I HEARD A COMMERCIAL.

CHAPTER 5 : THE CHRISTMAS HERO

Christmas is only a few days away. A photo shop down the street is decorated with lights...

WE WANTED TO MAKE A CHRISTMAS CARD FOR OUR FRIENDS WITH OUR PICTURE ON IT. SAM, OUR CAT, AND ME...

GREAT IDEA!

PLEASE JUST WAIT A FEW MINUTES WHILE I FINISH UP THESE PRINTS.

OKAY.

CAT.

MY NAME'S BRINA, YOUR'S?

FRED.

SO YOU'RE HERE FOR CHRISTMAS CARDS.

I HATE CHRISTMAS.

WHY DO YOU HATE IT? I LIKE IT A LOT!

ONE CHRISTMAS, SOME YEARS AGO, EVERYTHING... CHANGED...

"I WAS TRAINED BY THE FIRE DEPARTMENT. A RESCUE DOG, I WAS SO PROUD...

"WE WORKED IN A PLEASANT HILLY TOWN...

"UNFORTUNATELY, I'LL REMEMBER THAT CHRISTMAS FOR A LONG TIME. THERE WAS AN EARTHQUAKE, AND IN A FEW SHORT MINUTES, THE TOWN WAS GONE. OUR MISSION WAS TO FIND PEOPLE IN THE RUBBLE... AND RESCUE THEM.

"I STRAYED AWAY FROM MY COMPANIONS BECAUSE I SENSED A PRESENCE OF SOMEONE I KNEW...

I'M HERE!

"MR. BERTHOD WAS THE OWNER OF A PHOTO SHOP."

"BUT THEN..."

AUUUH!

"WE KEPT EACH OTHER COMPANY FOR MANY LONG HOURS..."

"... UNTIL MY COMPANIONS RESCUED US."

"I'D LOST THE USE OF MY HIND LEGS. MR. BERTHOD LOST HIS STORE."

"THE WORST CHRISTMAS EVER..."

"I COULD NO LONGER BE A RESCUE DOG. SO MR. BERTHOD DECIDED TO KEEP ME. TOGETHER WE MOVED TO THE CITY, FOR A NEW LIFE..."

... AND A NEW PHOTO SHOP?

YOU SEE, ONCE I WAS RESCUE DOG, BUT NOW I'M JUST A DISABLED DOG WHO'S NO LONGER GOOD FOR ANYTHING.

ALL SET. HEAD ON IN AND I CAN TAKE THE PICTURE.

COME ON, BRINA.

While posing for the photo, Brina can't stop thinking about Fred and his story...

How can she help bring back his smile?

Then: an idea!

YOUR CARDS WILL BE READY IN 24 HOURS.

SEE YOU TOMORROW.

LOOK, HONEY! IT'S STARTING TO SNOW!

"Perfect!," thinks Brina. With the snow, her plan will be more effective for... saving Fred.

A little while later, Brina leaps into action on the terrace.

She's sure she'll find someone there willing to help her...

HELLO, OLIVER.

I NEED YOU TO DO ME A FAVOR.

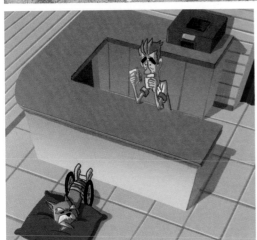

SCREECH!

WHAT IS HE DOING?!

?

WHAT'S GOING ON?

A... PARROT!

SCREECH!

HE'S STUCK IN THAT TREE!

THERE'S A STRAY CAT LOOKING TO GOBBLE IT UP TOO!

MEOWWW!

I WONDER HOW IT GOT THERE...

AND IT MUST BE SO SCARED, POOR THING!

Fred can't stay away from the scene for long...

Someone in danger is still someone in danger... even if they have wings instead of arms.

And a rescue dog, even if he has wheels instead of legs... is always still a rescue dog!

WOOF! WOOF!

FRED!

OOPS!

AAA...

... AH!

HE'S WARMING UP THE BIRD!

AMAZING!

It didn't matter how much time had passed: a rescue dog never forgets his training.

WHAT'S YOUR DOG DOING?

I HAVE NO IDEA.

THE PARROT'S WAKING UP!

FRED, YOU SAVED AN EXOTIC ANIMAL!

YOU'RE A HERO!

WHAT HAPPENED?

WE'VE GOT A HEROIC DOG IN OUR NEIGHBORHOOD!

BRAVO, FRED!

HERE, HAVE A BITE OF MY PIZZA.

A day later, it's time to pick up the Christmas cards...

WE'RE HOME!

THEY LOOK GOOD AND WE LOOK GOOD!

DID YOU KNOW THE PHOTO SHOP DOG WAS A HERO? YOU MET HIM THERE, BRINA.

THEY EVEN MENTIONED HIM IN THE PAPER.

CHRISTMAS HERO

OPEN

Chapter 6 : Hopping Hurricane

The hallway of Brina's apartment building...

A finger presses the doorbell...

BRRRRIIINNN

What new adventures await on the other side of the door?

HI, MARGRET, HEY, SAM.

I HAVE TO GO AWAY FOR A FEW DAYS AND I NEED SOMEONE TO KEEP AN EYE ON MY LITTLE TEDDY.

WHO IS IT?

OH, GINA, HELLO!

WOULD YOU WATCH HIM FOR ME?

The days pass without incident and the little bunny does nothing to worry the humans in the house.

LOOKING AFTER A RABBIT IS PRETTY EASY, HUH?

WE'RE GOING SHOPPING.

BE GOOD.

LET'S PARTY!

YAAAY!

HEY! I'M THE ONE WHO USUALLY MAKES A MESS!

STOP! YOU WANT TO STAY IN THIS HOME? YOU HAVE TO RESPECT HOW THINGS ARE DONE HERE.

?

EAT A LITTLE KIBBLE, DRINK A LITTLE WATER...

VISIT THE BALCONY TO CHASE AWAY INTRUDERS...

AND THEN A NICE NAP UNTIL MARGRET AND SAM RETURN.

OKAY...

?

Teddy isn't one to easily accept the rules of the house.

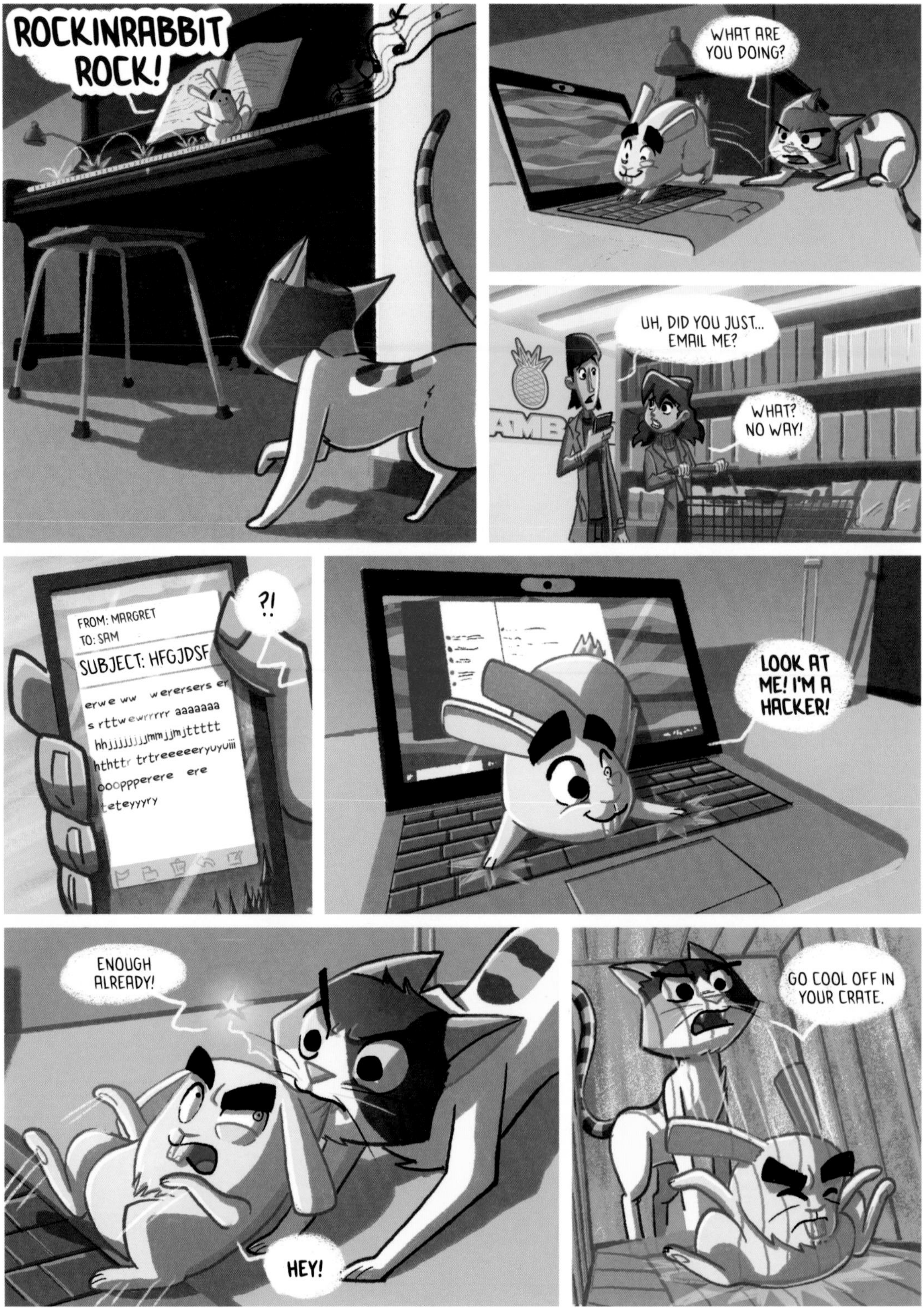
ROCKINRABBIT ROCK!
WHAT ARE YOU DOING?
UH, DID YOU JUST... EMAIL ME?
WHAT? NO WAY!
FROM: MARGRET
TO: SAM
SUBJECT: HFGJDSF
erwe ww wererser er
s rttwewrrrrr aaaaaaa
hhjjjjjjjjmmjjmjttttt
hthttr trtreeeeeryuyuiii
oooppperere ere
teteyyyry
?!
LOOK AT ME! I'M A HACKER!
ENOUGH ALREADY!
HEY!
GO COOL OFF IN YOUR CRATE.

FINALLY, A MOMENT OF PEAC--

OH, NO!

WHERE'D HE GO?

LOOK OUT FOR TUTANKHABUNNY, THE RABBITMUMMY!

!

Our adventurous feline has faced many dangers on the city streets and country roads...

... but she never would have thought...

STOP IT!

OOPS!

... she'd end up KO'd in her own broom closet.

Not satisfied with his mess, Teddy turns to the TV for entertainment..

click

911, WHAT'S YOUR EMERGENCY?

ARGH! BOOM! BANG BANG!

Bang! Bang!

...then the phone.

I HAVE TO BE CUNNING...

TEDDY?

AN APPLE?... I LOVE APPLES!

COME AND GET IT!

I'M HUNGRY!

!

THAT'S THAT...

HEY, HUH...?!

BRINA? TEDDY? WE'RE BACK!

BUT... WHAT HAPPENED HERE?

Bang! Boom!

BRINA, DID YOU DO THIS? YOU LOCKED TEDDY IN HIS CRATE TOO!

I DON'T THINK THIS IS HER FAULT.

THESE DON'T LOOK LIKE CAT BITES.

LOOK AT WHAT MY WEBCAM RECORDED.

THAT SOLVES THE MYSTERY OF THE CRAZY EMAIL.

SO IT WAS TEDDY WHO MADE THIS MESS!

SOMEONE'S AT THE DOOR... I'LL GET IT.

... YES?

SOMEONE HEARD GUN SHOTS AND CALLED US.

Gina's return is timely, although she has no idea what awaits her...

WHAT'S UP WITH ALL THESE EMERGENCY VEHICLES? I HOPE MY SWEET TEDDY IS SAFE.

HELLO, I'M BACK--

B-BUT...?

!

Chapter 7 : Follow the Bouncing Ball

Happiness...

... is a fleeting feeling.

When it's here, it seems endless.

But sometimes we're so busy playing with our own destiny...

... that happiness leaves the way it came: in a moment.

Sometimes happiness looks like a fluke, an imperfection...

And we drive it away, unrecognized...

But happiness does surprise us when we're not expecting it to...

It travels in strange ways...

It isn't bothered by dirt or mess...

If it goes away, it's up to us to find it...

Because once we experience it...

... we'll do anything to regain lost happiness.

Sometimes we're too busy planning for the future...

... or fighting with our neighbors...

... and happiness passes us by without anyone noticing.

Other times we definitely notice it!

And we're prepared to run any risk to seize it...

Sometimes, others can take our happiness away...

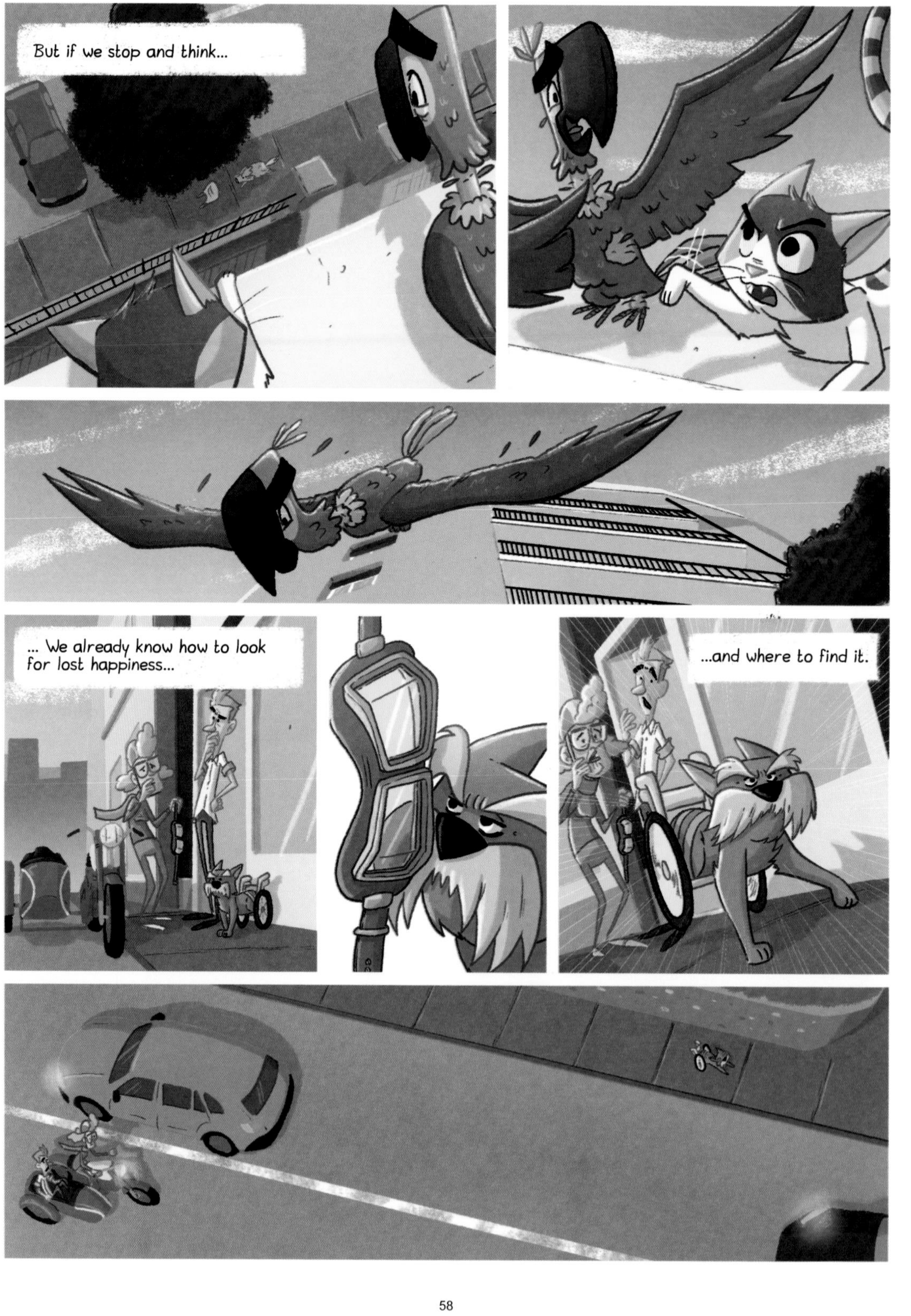
But if we stop and think...
... We already know how to look for lost happiness...
...and where to find it.

It's not about the daily fight for control...

Or waiting for a moment that may never come...

Happiness is in encounters. And in others...

It's in a bond between souls.

It's in the hearts of those who have the courage to embrace it, to find it...

When we do manage to seize happiness...

... It shines even more brightly if we share it with those who have lost it.

So once it's back in our hearts...

... we know we have to hold it close to us.

The sun shines all day and sets late: it's summer vacation again!

Brina, Margret, and Sam are happily packing their luggage, because...

...WE'RE OFF TO THE MOUNTAINS!

Everyone gets settled in their places...

... and the family heads off toward their favorite valley.

But not without first stopping to get supplies!

SHOULD WE GET COLD CUTS?

YOU KIDDING? WITH ALL THE MEAT WE CAN FIND IN HIGH HOPES HILLS?

GRANDMA, LOOK AT THE PRETTY CAT!

A mischievous hand...

... loosens the door of the cat carrier.

A worker is moving some cases of fish...

... right when a poorly placed bag opens the door to escape.

And we all know that for a cat, the smell of fish is a strong temptation to resist...

... too strong.

THE SCENT IS COMING FROM OVER THERE.

I'VE LOST THE TRAIL... LET'S TRY IN HERE.

!

WE'RE FINALLY READY TO GO.

A sad fate for Brina, locked in a truck while her humans, unaware of her absence, head out on vacation...

MEOOOW!

But fate can help cats too, in the shape of a pigeon, Peter, who's looking for food nearby.

MEOOOW!

I THINK I KNOW THAT MEOW.

BRINA, THAT YOU?

PETER! HELP ME OUT OF HERE, PLEASE!

➝GNNN...➝ I CAN'T DO IT!

HANG TIGHT... I'LL BE RIGHT BACK.

"Why aren't Sam and Margret rescuing me?"

"Didn't they notice I'm not there?"

These questions fill the cat's mind as she anxiously waits in the dark.

SEE, I HAD TO CALL A FEW FOLKS FOR HELP.

THANKS, FRIENDS!

THEIR CAR'S NOT HERE ...THEY LEFT WITHOUT ME.

HOW CAN I EVER GET TO THEM NOW?

I HAVE AN IDEA...

MY OWNER TOOK ME ON A TRIP ONCE... IF I RECALL CORRECTLY, THE STATION IS OVER THIS WAY.

I'LL MONITOR THE SITUATION FROM ABOVE.

WE NEED TO FIND THE BUS STATION.

MAYBE WE CAN FIND ONE THAT'LL TAKE HER TO WHERE HER HUMANS ARE GOING.

I'LL FOLLOW YOU.

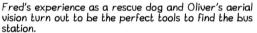

Fred's experience as a rescue dog and Oliver's aerial vision turn out to be the perfect tools to find the bus station.

THERE!

WHICH IS THE RIGHT BUS?

JUST A MINUTE... I RECOGNIZE THIS PLACE!

HIGH HOPE HILLS

THAT'S HIGH HOPE HILLS, I'M SURE OF IT!

WE NEED TO GET YOU ON BOARD.

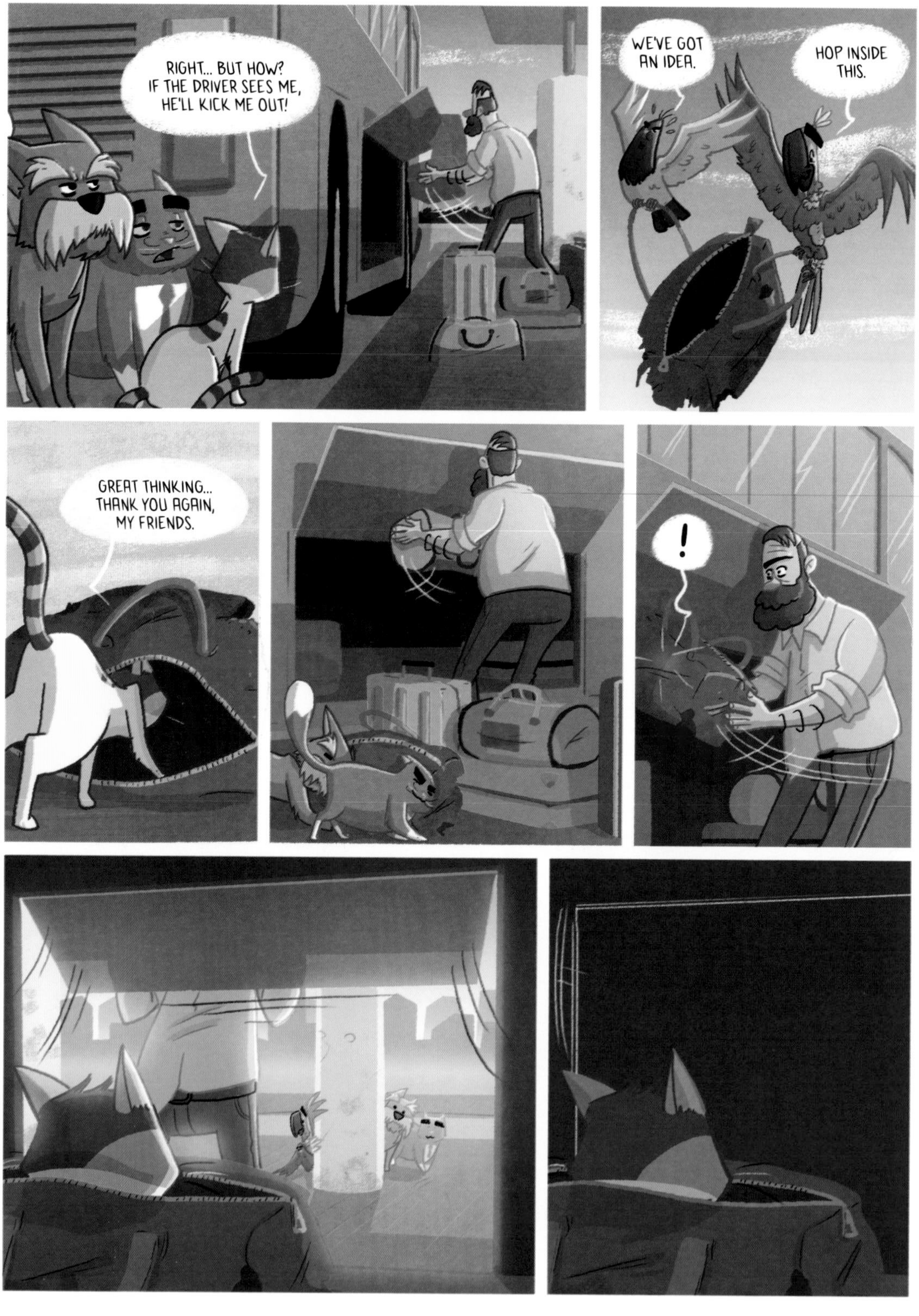
RIGHT... BUT HOW? IF THE DRIVER SEES ME, HE'LL KICK ME OUT!
WE'VE GOT AN IDEA.
HOP INSIDE THIS.
GREAT THINKING... THANK YOU AGAIN, MY FRIENDS.
!

As the bus leaves for its destination, Brina wonders why the four animals did all they could to help her...

But then she remembers the time she helped Peter get out of the apartment building...

... and when she helped Fred feel proud of himself again, and the day she freed Oliver.

That's why her friends helped her when she was in trouble!

The journey seems to last forever, but the bus finally reaches its destination.

WHAT THE--?!

OUR HOUSE SHOULD BE AROUND HERE SOMEWHERE.

Her feline sense of smell has brought her to the rental house once again. Now she knows where to go!

Brina reaches her humans at just the right moment.

BRINA DIDN'T MAKE A PEEP THE WHOLE TRIP.

DID YOU SLEEP THE WHOLE TIME? LAZYBONES!

WE'RE BACK IN THE MOUNTAINS, BRINA!

WE'RE GOING TO HAVE LOTS OF FUN!

Brina's back with her family, thanks to the help of a pigeon, a dog, a parrot, and a stray cat.

Because this is today's discovery: the good you've done along the way comes back to you right when you need it the most.

Just like a cat...

It's time for Brina, Margret, and Sam to get a little R&R at their mountain home.

UMM... THERE'S NO POWER!

Clic

OF COURSE NOT! THE CIRCUIT BREAKER FOR THE APARTMENT IS BROKEN... BUT I CAN'T OPEN IT TO FIX IT!

OH, HELLO, HUBERT...

SOMEONE STOLE MY SCREWDRIVER, FLASHLIGHT, AND WORK GLOVES FROM THE SHED! CAN YOU BELIEVE IT?

BUT WHO COULD HAVE DONE THAT?

ALL I KNOW IS I FOUND CAT PRINTS... TWO GUESSES WHO THE PURR-P IS?

THAT'S IMPOSSIBLE WE JUST GOT HERE!

I CAN'T BELIEVE HUBERT'S ACCUSING US OF THEFT LIKE THAT.

BRINA WANTS TO GO OUT...

MEOW!

IF YOU WANT TO GO OUT, YOU NEED TO WEAR YOUR HARNESS.

ARE YOU SURE? YOU KNOW SHE LIKES TO RUN AWAY...

THAT'S WHY I HAD THIS TAG MADE.

IF SOMEONE FINDS HER FAR FROM HOME, OUR CONTACT INFO IS ALL RIGHT HERE.

ANYWAY, SHE'S NOT A KITTY ANYMORE. I'M SURE SHE'LL COME HOME BY NIGHTTIME.

I HOPE YOU'RE RIGHT.

Brina's first thought is to go looking for the other cats.

The cats she'd once been in a gang with.

LOOK WHO'S COMING, VESPUCCI.

I THINK WE KNOW THAT CAT, GABRIELLE... DON'T WE?

IT'S BRINA, THE CITY CAT!

AND YOU WERE ONCE STRAY CATS.

WE'VE ADOPTED THE HUMANS THAT LIVE HERE. ALL IN ALL, THEY SERVE AND REVERE US.

PETER!

THERE'S FOOD MISSING... AGAIN! I BET YOUR CATS DID IT!

BUT, MA...?

WHAT'S GOING ON?

IT'S THAT OLD WITCH...SOMEONE'S BEEN STEALING FROM HER PANTRY FOR DAYS AND SHE BLAMES US.

BUT WE DIDN'T DO ANYTHING! HONEST!

A MYSTERIOUS CAT'S BEEN ROAMING AROUND THESE PARTS...

COULD THEY HAVE STOLEN HUBERT'S TOOLS TOO?

"ONE TIME I CAUGHT A GLIMPSE OF HIM... HE WAS WHITE OR GRAY... HE WAS RUNNING WITH A SPOON IN HIS MOUTH AND THE TIP OF HIS TAIL WAS MISSING."

THAT DEFINITELY HAS TO BE CUTTAIL, THE PIRATE CAT.

CUTTAIL?

"YES, WHEN I WAS A KITTEN, MY MOTHER USED TO TELL ME HIS STORY...

"CUTTAIL LIVED ON A BUCCANEER'S GALLEON...

"LIKE ALL PIRATES, HE HAD HIS TREASURE TOO...

"HIS JOB ON SHIP WAS HUNTING THE MICE...

"BUT ONE TERRIBLE DAY, HE BECAME THE PREY OF HIS WORST ENEMIES... SHARKS!

"SINCE THEN, THE GHOST OF CUTTAIL WANDERS THROUGH THE VALLEYS, STEALING WHATEVER HE CAN TO REBUILD HIS TREASURE."

THAT... THAT'S FRIGHTENING!

A MOUNTAIN PIRATE GHOST?

YOU'RE NOT CONVINCED BY THE STORY, BRINA?

NOT VERY MUCH...

BUT THE ONLY WAY TO FIND OUT THE TRUTH IS TO FIND HIM AND CATCH HIM.

WHO IS IT? DON'T YOU WANT TO FIND OUT WHO THE MYSTERIOUS THIEF IS TOO?

I COULD LIVE WITH NOT KNOWING!

OKAY THEN. LET'S TAKE A STROLL AROUND THE TOWN AND SEE IF WE FIND ANY TRACE OF HIM.

But the gang of the feline sun isn't complete: it's still missing one member...

BRINA! MY FRIEND!

ATOM! WE NEED YOUR HELP!

OH... THEY'RE HERE TOO.

WE'RE LOOKING FOR A MYSTERIOUS CAT WHO'S BEEN STEALING FROM THE HOUSES AROUND HERE...

I KNOW EXACTLY WHAT YOU'RE TALKING ABOUT...

BUT I WON'T SAY ANYTHING AS LONG AS VESPUCCI'S HERE... HE'S NOT MY FRIEND.

DON'T YOU HAVE ANYTHING TO SAY?

ME? I DON'T EVEN KNOW WHY HE'S MAD AT ME.

"I DO. WHEN YOU WERE HEAD OF OUR GANG YOU WERE VERY AGGRESSIVE, ESPECIALLY WITH ATOM."

THAT'S TRUE... MAYBE I DID GO TOO FAR.

WHAT DO YOU SAY, ATOM... DOES THAT COUNT AS AN APOLOGY?

"WELL, OKAY...HERE'S WHAT I SAW. A HUGE WHITE CAT WAS RUNNING THROUGH THE FOREST!"

SEE? IT HAD TO HAVE BEEN THE PIRATE CAT.

PIRATE? I DON'T THINK SO.

"IT LOOKED MORE LIKE A YETI TO ME..."

A SUPER-SCARY YETI-CAT!

THAT'S EVEN MORE FRIGHTENING THAN A GHOST PIRATE!

GHOSTS... YETIS... WHO KNOWS WHAT TO BELIEVE ANYMORE?

THAT'S WHY WE HAVE TO SOLVE THIS MYSTERY. ALL OF US TOGETHER. WHAT DO YOU SAY?

I...

THAT'S...

OH, OKAY, FINE.

WHY NOT?

I'M IN!

GREAT!

WE ARE...
THE GANG OF THE FELINE SUN!

So the five friends venture forth together into the woods...

...looking for any sign that can lead them to the mysterious feline that has thrown the town into such disarray.

HERE ARE SOME TRACKS...

BUT SOMEONE SCRATCHED THEIR NAILS ON THIS TREE.

THEY MUST HAVE REALLY LONG NAILS!

I TOLD YOU IT WAS A YETI!

WH-WHAT WAS THAT?

SOUNDED HALFWAY BETWEEN A MEOW AND A ROAR!

I THINK WE'RE CLOSE. WE COULD TRY SPLITTING UP TO LOOK.

GOOD IDEA, BRINA. WHOEVER BUMPS INTO CUTTAIL FIRST WILL WARN THE OTHERS.

I CAN SMELL A CAT, BUT IT'S NOT ONE OF MY PALS.

IN FACT, IT'S THE SCENT OF... THE WILD.

AND THAT LOOKS LIKE A LAIR.

Brina doesn't like tight spaces and the entrance to the cave doesn't bode well...

... but inside, there's something that proves her detective work paid off.

HEY, YOU! WHAT DO YOU WANT?

!

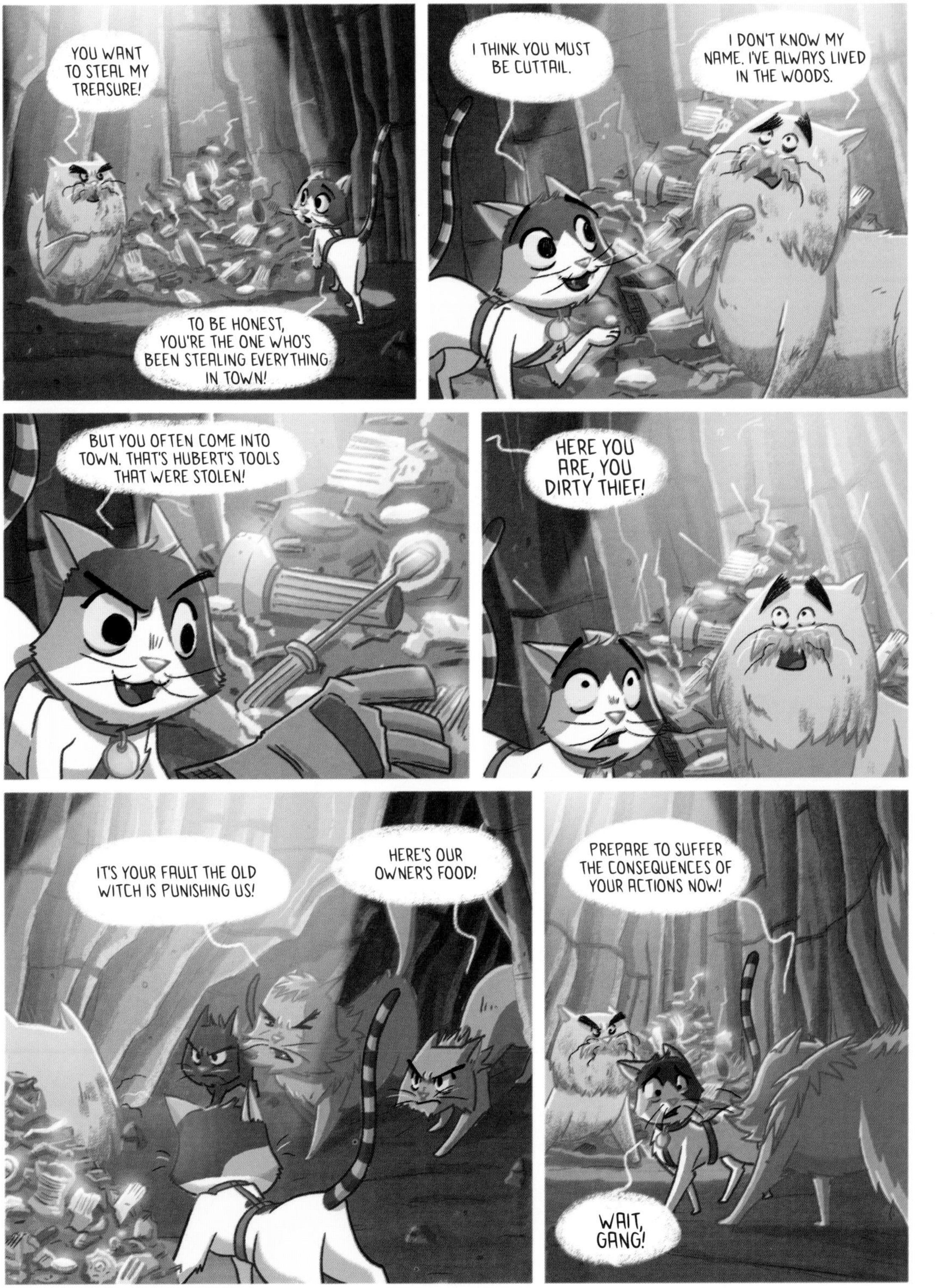
YOU WANT TO STEAL MY TREASURE!
TO BE HONEST, YOU'RE THE ONE WHO'S BEEN STEALING EVERYTHING IN TOWN!
I THINK YOU MUST BE CUTTAIL.
I DON'T KNOW MY NAME. I'VE ALWAYS LIVED IN THE WOODS.
BUT YOU OFTEN COME INTO TOWN. THAT'S HUBERT'S TOOLS THAT WERE STOLEN!
HERE YOU ARE, YOU DIRTY THIEF!
IT'S YOUR FAULT THE OLD WITCH IS PUNISHING US!
HERE'S OUR OWNER'S FOOD!
PREPARE TO SUFFER THE CONSEQUENCES OF YOUR ACTIONS NOW!
WAIT, GANG!

HE'S JUST A LITTLE WILD, BUT HE DOESN'T SEEM BAD TO ME.

LISTEN, CUTTAIL... IF YOU DON'T STOP STEALING, ALL THE CATS IN THE HIGH HOPE HILLS VALLEY WILL GET BLAMED.

I UNDERSTAND.

ONE DAY, LOTS AND LOTS OF CATS MAY COME HERE, AND THEY'LL BE REALLY VERY ANGRY ABOUT YOUR BEHAVIOR.

OKAY, THEN. I'LL STOP TAKING OTHER PEOPLE'S THINGS.

GOOD!

THAT MEANS I CAN TAKE BACK HUBERT'S TOOLS WITH ME?

NO! THESE THINGS ARE MINE NOW!

I'LL ONLY GIVE THEM BACK IF I CAN HAVE SOMETHING IN EXCHANGE.

I DON'T HAVE ANYTHING TO GIVE YOU...

THE TAG AROUND YOUR NECK... HOW SHINY... LOOKS VERY, VERY VALUABLE.

BUT MARGRET AND SAM GAVE IT TO ME!

STILL, HUBERT SEEMED SO ANGRY AT US...

OKAY THEN. I'LL GIVE YOU THE TAG, BUT IN RETURN, I WANT BACK THE SCREWDRIVER, FLASHLIGHT, AND GLOVES...

COUNT ME IN.

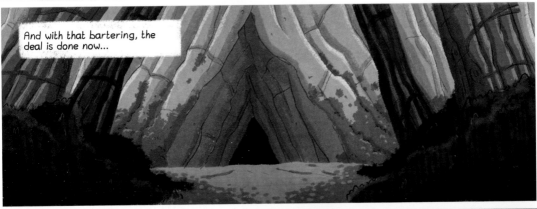
And with that bartering, the deal is done now...

Just in time before darkness falls on the evening sky over High Hope Hills and the peaks overlooking the valley...

So all that's left to do to restore peace in the neighborhood is to bring Hubert back his tools.

After that, Brina goes back home so that she won't worry her humans... or maybe because it's time for kibble?

SEE? I TOLD YOU SO!

WELL DONE!

BUT HER TAG IS MISSING...

OH, WELL. THE IMPORTANT THING IS SHE'S LEARNED TO COME HOME BY NIGHTTIME.

AND BECAUSE THE POWER'S STILL-- HUH!

IT'S BACK ON!

SOMEONE BROUGHT BACK MY TOOLS. I FIXED THE CIRCUIT BREAKER.

WHAT?!

YOU GAVE AWAY SOME OF THE TREASURE WITHOUT MY PERMISSION?!

BUT I GOT THIS SHINY TAG IN EXCHANGE.

AH!

SORRY I DOUBTED YOU, DESCENDANT... THIS OBJECT IS VERY VALUABLE, INDEED.

IT DESERVES AN HONORABLE SPOT IN MY TREASURE...

THE TREASURE OF **CUTTAIL** THE PIRATE CAT!

WATCH OUT FOR PAPERCUTZ

Welcome to the second slightly sentimental, self-reflecting BRINA THE CAT graphic novel, by writer Giorgio Salati, writer, and Christian Cornia, artist, from Papercutz, those crazy cat-video connoisseurs dedicated to publishing great graphic novels for all ages. I'm Jim Salicrup, the Editor-in-Chief and Keeper of the Kitty Litter. In BRINA THE CAT #1 (which is still available at libraries and booksellers everywhere), I told how cat-crazy we are at Papercutz and listed many of the Papercutz graphic novels that featured our favorite felines. Well, in the interest of equal time for canines, we wanted to mention there's an absolutely adorable little doggie in an exciting new series available from Papercutz right now. The dog's name is Dogmatix, and the series is called ASTERIX. It's a really big deal that Papercutz is publishing it, as ASTERIX is one of the biggest-selling graphic novel series in the world. This was big news and was even reported in *The New York Times* and *The Hollywood Reporter*. But regarding Dogmatix, while he does appear briefly—for one whole panel—in ASTERIX #1, it isn't until ASTERIX #2, where he starts to play a bigger role in the series. Now, some of you may not have heard of this Asterix fella, so let's take a quick journey in the Papercutz time machine…

We're back in the year 50 BC in the ancient country of Gaul, located where France, Belgium, and the Southern Netherlands are today. All of Gaul has been conquered by the Romans… well, not all of it. One tiny village, inhabited by indomitable Gauls, resists the invaders again and again. That doesn't make it easy for the garrisons of Roman soldiers surrounding the village in fortified camps.So, how's it possible that a small village can hold its own against the mighty Roman Empire?
The answer is this guy…

This is **Asterix**. A shrewd, little warrior of keen intellect… and superhuman strength. Asterix gets his superhuman strength from a magic potion. But he's not alone.

Obelix is Asterix's inseparable friend. He too has superhuman strength. He's a menhir (tall, upright stone monuments) deliveryman, he loves eating wild boar and getting into brawls. Obelix is always ready to drop everything to go off on a new adventure with Asterix. His constant companion (starting with ASTERIX #2) is **Dogmatix,** the only known canine ecologist, who howls with despair when a tree is cut down.

While we're here, we may as well meet a few other Gauls…
Panoramix, the village's venerable Druid, gathers mistletoe and prepares magic potions. His greatest success is the power potion. When a villager drinks this magical elixir he or she is temporarily granted super-strength. This is just one of the Druid's potions! And now you know why this small village can survive, despite seemingly impossible odds.

Cacofonix is the bard—the village poet. Opinions about his talents are divided: he thinks he's awesome, everybody else think he's awful, but when he doesn't sing anything, he's a cheerful companion and well-liked…

Vitalstatistix, finally, is the village's chief. Majestic, courageous, and irritable, the old warrior is respected by his men and feared by his enemies. Vitalstatistix has only one fear: that the sky will fall on his head but, as he says himself, "That'll be the day!"

There are plenty more characters around here, but you've met enough for now. It's time we get back to the palatial Papercutz offices and wrap this up. Now, where did we park our time machine? Oh, there it is! We're back. Of course, you may find dogs in other Papercutz titles—Charles in THE LOUD HOUSE and Puppy in THE SMURFS, for just a couple example — but we're so excited about ASTERIX, we couldn't resist sharing the news with you. But to prove we still love cats, take a look at the special preview of CAT & CAT #1 "Girl Meets Cat," by Cazenove, Richez, and Ramon on the following pages. It's the fun story of Cat (short for Catherine), her dad, and their newly adopted cat, Sushi. If you love cats, you'll love CAT & CAT. And if you love Brina, be sure not to miss the next BRINA THE CAT graphic novel coming your way soon.

Thanks,

JIM

STAY IN TOUCH!
EMAIL: salicrup@papercutz.com
WEB: papercutz.com
TWITTER: @papercutzgn
INSTAGRAM: @papercutzgn
FACEBOOK: PAPERCUTZGRAPHICNOVELS
FAN MAIL: Papercutz, 160 Broadway,
                Suite 700, East Wing
                New York, NY 10038

Here's a special preview of **Cat & Cat #1 "Girl Meets Cat"...**

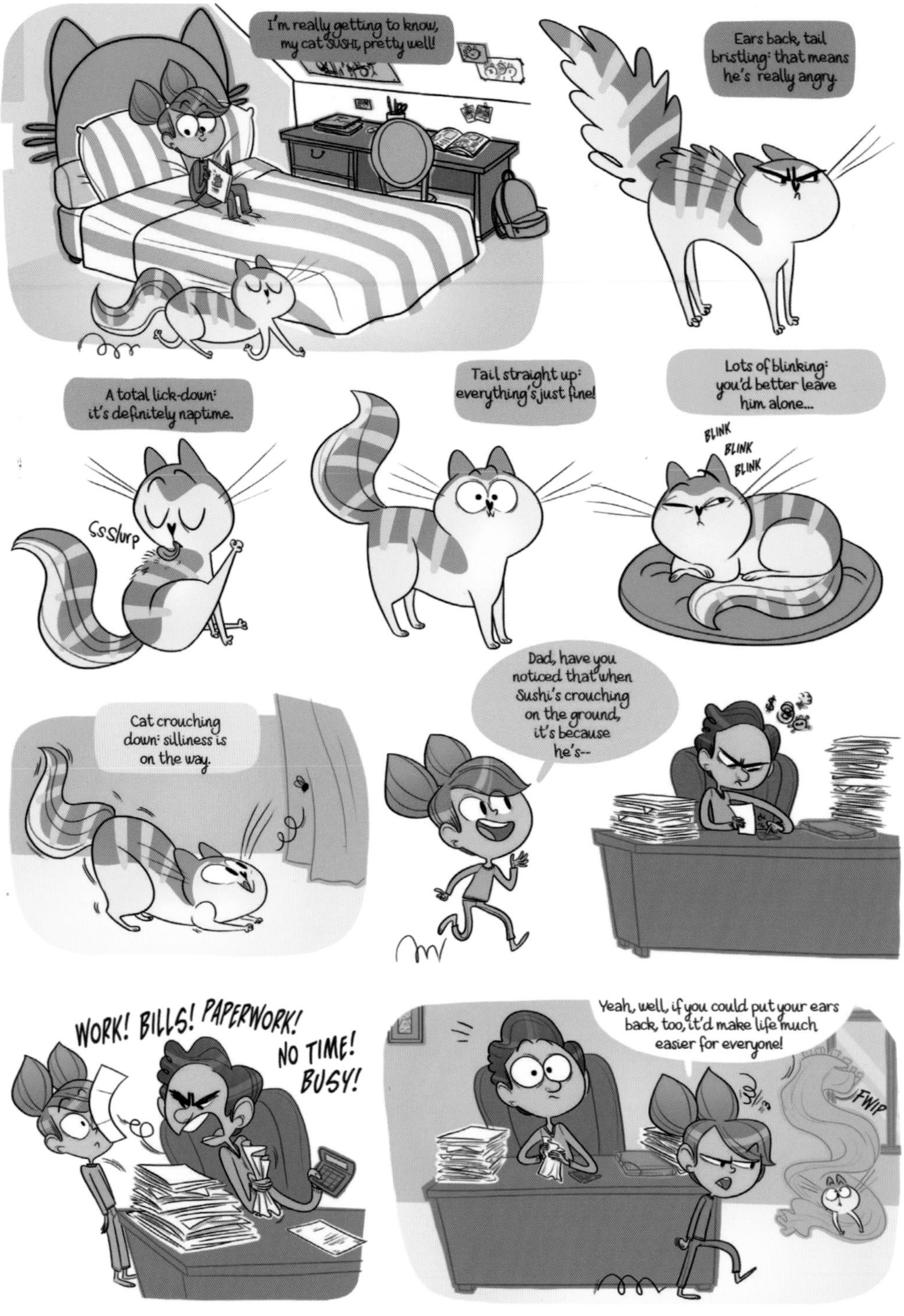
I'm really getting to know, my cat SUSHI, pretty well!
Ears back, tail bristling: that means he's really angry.
A total lick-down: it's definitely naptime.
SSSLURP
Tail straight up: everything's just fine!
Lots of blinking: you'd better leave him alone...
BLINK
BLINK
BLINK
Cat crouching down: silliness is on the way.
Dad, have you noticed that when Sushi's crouching on the ground, it's because he's--
WORK! BILLS! PAPERWORK!
NO TIME! BUSY!
Yeah, well, if you could put your ears back, too, it'd make life much easier for everyone!
FWIP

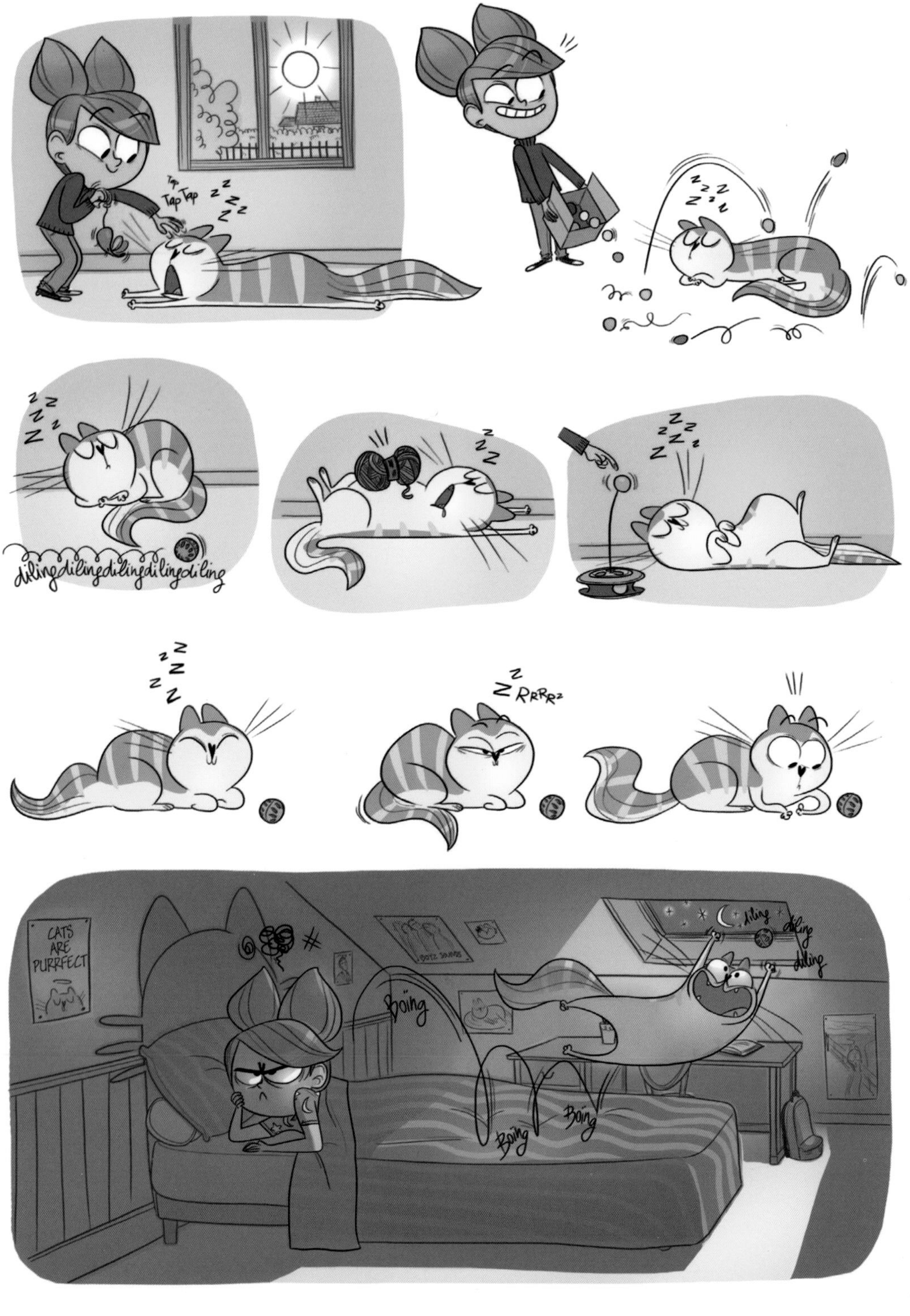
Tap
Tap Tap
Z Z Z
Z Z Z
Z Z Z
dilingdilingdilingdilingdiling
Z Z Z
Z Z Z
Z Z Z
Z RRRRz
CATS ARE PURRFECT
Boing
diling
diling
diling
Boing
Boing

Cat & Cat

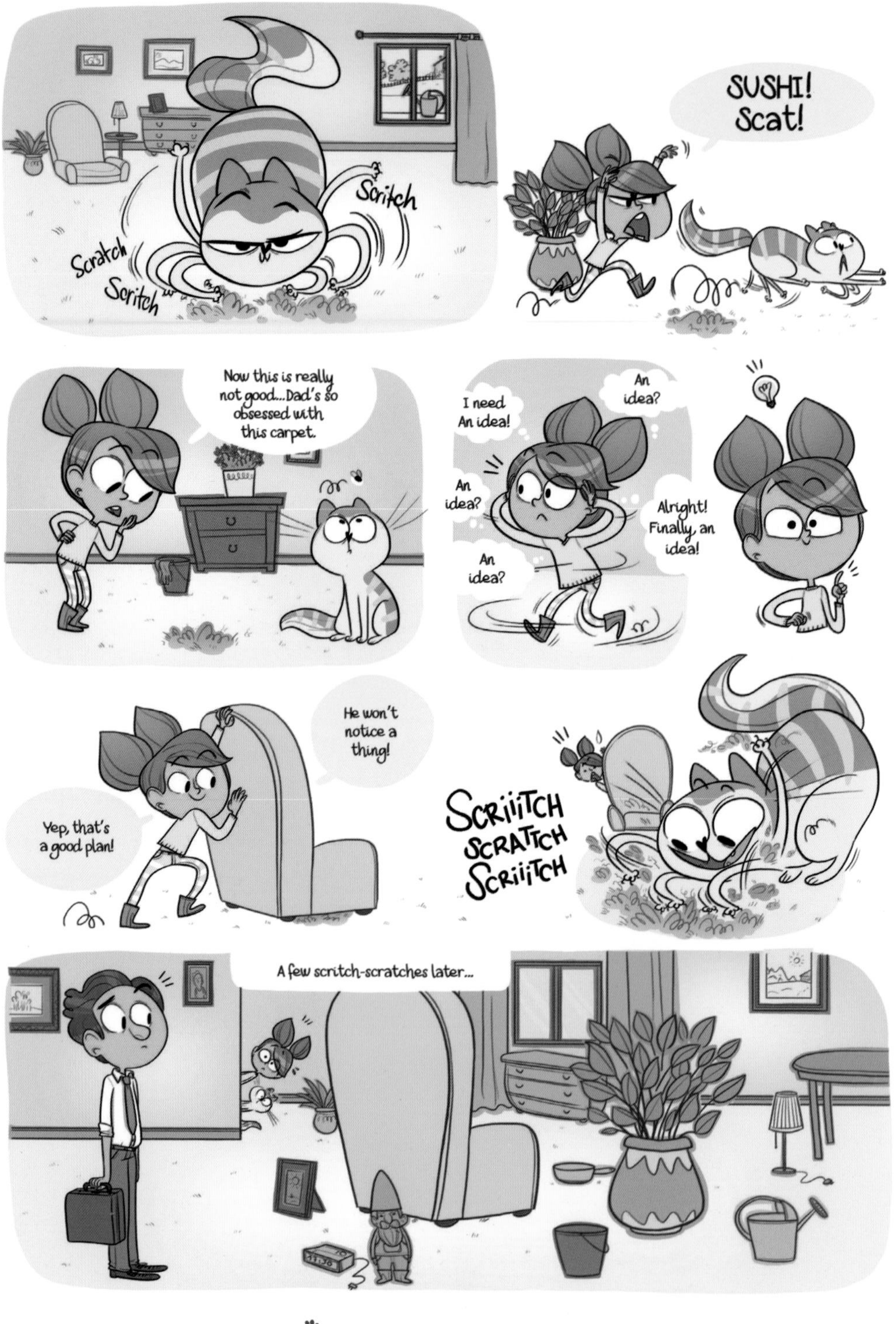
Scratch
Scritch
Scritch
SUSHI! Scat!
Now this is really not good...Dad's so obsessed with this carpet.
I need An idea!
An idea?
An idea?
An idea?
Alright! Finally, an idea!
Yep, that's a good plan!
He won't notice a thing!
SCRIIITCH
SCRATTCH
SCRIIITCH
A few scritch-scratches later...

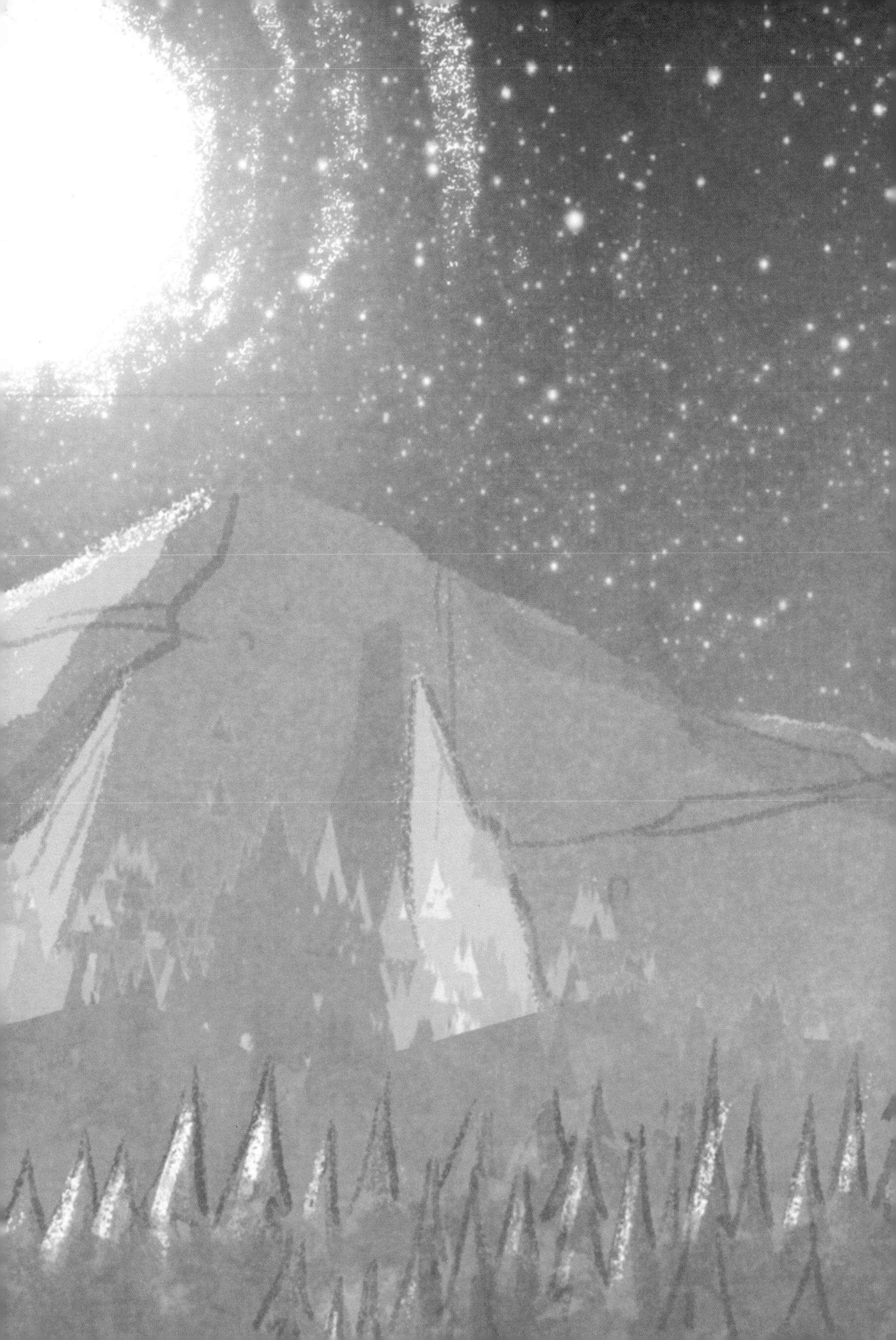